$16.95

AUTHOR Vic Parker

TITLE Traditional Tales from Norse Lands

BORROWER'S NAME

DATE DUE

214-B

TRADITIONAL TALES
from

NORSE LANDS

Vic Parker

Based on myths and legends retold by
Philip Ardagh

Illustrated by
Stephen May

Thameside Press

Distributed in the United States by
Smart Apple Media
1980 Lookout Drive
North Mankato, MN 56003

Printed in Singapore

Library of Congress Cataloging-in-Publication Data
Parker, Vic.
   Norse lands / by Vic Parker.
      p. cm.—(Traditional tales from around the world)
   Summary: A collection of tales relating the exploits and
   adventures of the gods and heroes of Norse mythology.
   ISBN 1-929298-73-0
      1. Mythology, Norse—Juvenile literature. [1. Mythology,
   Norse.] I. Title. II. Series.

BL860 .P37 2000
398.2'0948'01—dc21   00-022748

9 8 7 6 5 4 3 2 1

Editor: Stephanie Turnbull
Designer: Zoë Quayle
Educational consultant: Margaret Bellwood

Contents

The Norse Lands 4

Thor and the Giants 7

The Curse of the Ring 13

Tyr the Hero 19

Gerda the Beautiful 25

Thor's Lost Hammer 29

A Deadly Trick 35

Loki's Punishment 41

Index 48

THE NORSE LANDS

**The stories in this book were first told by the Norse people.
These folk lived over one thousand years ago in the cold
lands near the top of the world—Norway, Sweden,
Denmark, and Iceland.**

In these countries it is winter for most of the year. The ground
is covered with snow and ice, and the nights are long and dark.
The Norse people had to be brave to survive. They had to be
tough enough to build strong homes, bold enough to sail across
stormy seas, and fierce enough to fight against wolves and raiders.
These heroic warriors became known as the Vikings.

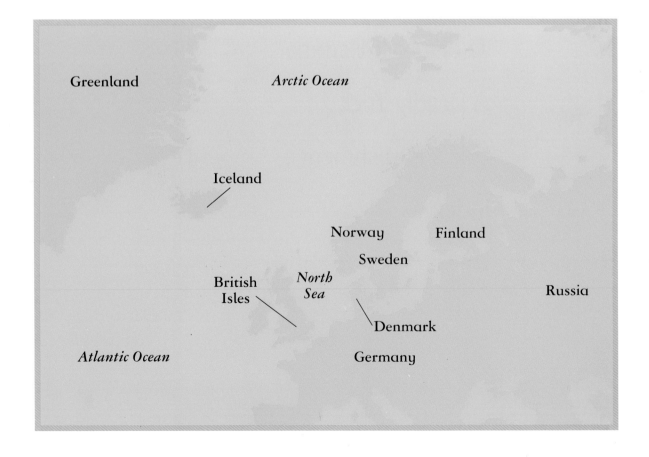

The Norse people thought that it wasn't just humans like themselves who lived in the universe. There were gods, giants, dwarfs, and elves, and all sorts of other beings too. Each type of creature had its own world to live in.

There were nine Norse worlds, held in place by a mighty tree, the Tree of Life. At the top of the tree, the stars sparkled and the birds flew. At the bottom of the tree, a terrible dragon called Nidhogg gnawed on the roots. A squirrel called Ratatosk ran busily up and down between the branches and the dragon.

Norse people believed that their world of Midgard was linked to the gods' world of Asgard by a rainbow bridge. The middle worlds were circled by a huge sea-serpent called Jormungand.

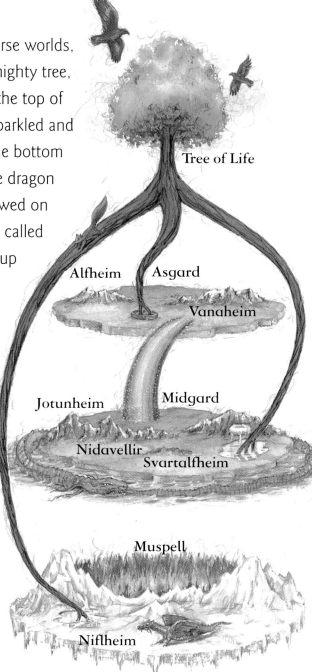

Tree of Life

Alfheim   Asgard

Vanaheim

Jotunheim   Midgard

Nidavellir
Svartalfheim

Muspell

Niflheim

Upper worlds:

Alfheim
The land of the light elves.

Asgard
The land of the warrior gods and goddesses.

Vanaheim
The land of the gods and goddesses who make everything grow.

Middle worlds:

Jotunheim
The land of the giants.

Midgard
The land of humans.

Nidavellir
The land of the dwarfs.

Svartalfheim
The land of the dark elves.

Lower worlds:

Muspell
A land of fire.

Niflheim
The kingdom of the dead.

5

THOR AND THE GIANTS

During the winter, people in the world of Midgard huddle around their fires and tell each other tales of their heroes, the gods and goddesses from the magical land of Asgard. These superhuman beings are the bravest of warriors.

The strongest of them all is Thor, the god of thunder. He has an enchanted hammer called Mjollnir. When he throws this, it kills anything it touches. The mighty thunder god races across the universe in a war chariot pulled by two fierce goats. And Thor doesn't wait for his enemies to come to him—he goes out and finds them.

Once, Thor dared to travel deep into the land of the giants. He took his friend Loki and two servant children called Thialfi and Roskva. They braved many dangers and finally reached an enormous hall—the home of the king of the giants. Thor did not bother to knock. He used his great strength to push open the huge doors, and he and his friends marched straight in.

The king of the giants and his giant chiefs roared with laughter at these strangers, who seemed so tiny.

"Look, it's the mighty Thor! Be careful or we might squash him!" they teased.

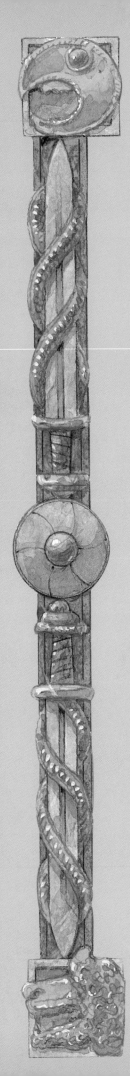

"And he's brought some funny little friends," they guffawed. "How sweet!"

"Enough!" shouted Thor, waving his famous hammer. At once, the giants fell silent.

"Where is your respect?" Thor thundered.

"If you want our respect, you will have to earn it," the king of the giants growled. "Take on my giants in any challenge you like. I bet you can't win even once."

Thor flexed his muscles.

"We accept!" he announced. "Prepare to be beaten."

The giants jeered and stamped their feet until the stone floor shook.

"How about an eating competition?" challenged Loki, Thor's friend. Loki was half-god, half-giant, and he was extremely hungry after the long journey.

"Excellent!" boomed the king of the giants.

He nodded to his servants and they brought in dish after dish of delicious-looking food and placed them on a long, long table. Loki stood at one end, his mouth watering. A giant stood at the other, licking his lips. The king gave the signal and the eating contest began.

Loki was a blur of speed. He wolfed down all the food from his end of the table in an instant and stood back in triumph, wiping his mouth.

But when he looked up at his rival, he was amazed. The giant had swallowed the plates and all the bones too!

"We won!" the giants whooped and cheered.

"I'll show these big brutes!" whispered Thor's servant Thialfi to his sister Roskva. He pushed his way forward.

"Who will race me?" he cried.

The king of the giants laughed so hard, he nearly fell off his chair. A young giant runner lined up with Thialfi.

"GO!" yelled Thor.

Thialfi shot forward like an arrow—only to see the giants lifting their champion high onto their shoulders. He had already reached the finishing line!

Thor thumped his fist on a chair and split it in two.

"King of the giants, I challenge you to a drinking match!" he bellowed furiously.

"Wonderful!" grinned the king, and handed Thor a huge drinking horn.

Glug—glug—glug ... Thor drank until his arms were aching, his stomach bursting, his chest gasping for air— and finally gave in. He just could not finish the drink.

Thor's hair bristled with anger.

"I won't embarrass you more by showing you how much *I* can drink," sneered the king. "Why don't you try something easier, like lifting up that little cat?"

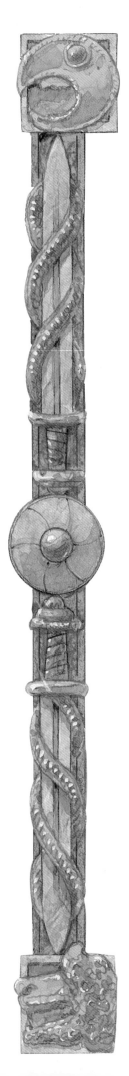

Fuming, the thunder god strode over to the cat, who lay asleep by the fireplace. But even though Thor huffed and puffed, grunted and groaned, he could not lift one paw.

Fury flashed in Thor's eyes like lightning.

"One more chance!" he raged. "Bring out whoever you like. No matter how big they are, I'll wrestle them to the ground if it's the last thing I do!"

"What about my old nanny?" the king said, and a shaking, bent-over woman hobbled out.

"I can't fight a wrinkled old lady!" Thor gasped.

"Well, if she's too much for you ..." teased the king.

At that, Thor hurled himself at the elderly woman. To his horror, she stood her ground and gripped him like steel. She grappled the struggling Thor to his knees without even pausing for breath.

The thunder god and his friends had had enough. Red-faced, they allowed the king to lead them back to the border of his kingdom.

"Before we say goodbye," said the king of the giants, "I have something to tell you. I used magic to trick you. Nothing was as it seemed. Loki ate fast, but his opponent was really Fire, which devours everything in its path. Your servant Thialfi was a swift runner, but he raced against Thought—the fastest thing in the world.

As for you, Thor, that horn was filled with the ocean, but you drank so much that you created the tides. And we trembled when you tried to lift my cat, for it was really the great serpent that circles the whole universe. As for my nanny, she was actually Old Age itself. You put up an incredible fight, but old age beats everyone in the end."

Thor's face was dark as a thundercloud. He didn't know whether to feel foolish, angry, or proud.

"You have shown us what mighty things the gods can do," said the king. "Now go away and leave us alone."

Thor and his friends made their way back to Asgard. They had won more glory to their names. But they never forgot the sound of giant laughter ringing in their ears.

THE CURSE
OF THE RING

Now and then, the warrior gods and goddesses like
to leave their lovely home, Asgard, and go exploring
to the worlds below. They enjoy mingling with humans,
and they often walk through the land of Midgard in
disguise. Sometimes they boldly visit the giants in
their land of Jotunheim. But the gods and goddesses
usually keep out of the way of dwarfs. For dwarfs love
gold, and dwarf gold always means trouble....

One sunny day, three gods were enjoying a walk
along a river. They were Odin, the chief of the gods,
Hoenir, his brother, and Loki, the mischief-making
god. As they strolled along, they saw an otter creep
out from the riverbank and catch a leaping salmon
between its paws.

"How quick and cunning that animal is!" gasped
Hoenir, gazing at the otter.

"And how hungry I am!" replied Odin, his eyes
on the fish.

"But I'm the most quick and cunning and hungry
of all!" cried Loki, throwing a stone at the otter and
knocking it dead.

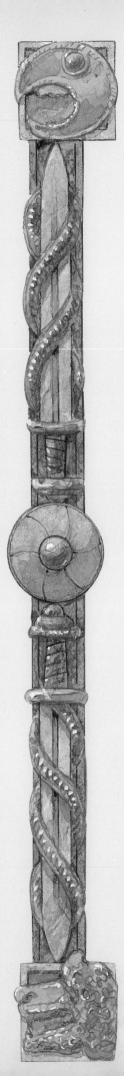

A few minutes later Odin had built a fire, Hoenir was cooking the salmon, and Loki was skinning the otter.

As the delicious smell of roasting fish filled the air, a furious little man appeared as if from nowhere. His face was purple and he looked about to explode with anger. He jumped up and down, shaking his fists and yelling so wildly that the gods couldn't understand a word he said.

"Murderers!" they finally made out.

Odin stood up at once.

"Be careful who you call a murderer," he said calmly. 'You don't know who you might be insulting.'

"I really don't care!" spluttered the short, round man. "I am Hreidmar, the king of the dwarfs, and that was one of my sons you just killed!"

He pointed angrily at the otter skin Loki was holding, and the gods realized with horror what had happened. Dwarf magic was very strong, and some dwarfs were able to change shape. Instead of catching an otter, Loki had killed a dwarf prince!

"You will die for your mistake," came a cold voice from behind the gods.

They spun around to find that two more furious dwarfs had appeared. They were the king's other sons, Fafnir and Regin, and their swords were drawn and ready.

"Wait!" Odin commanded. "If you kill us, you won't be any better off. There must be some way we can repay you instead."

A greedy glint sparkled in the king's beady eyes.

"Hmmm," he thought for a moment. "Bring me enough gold to fill the otter skin and enough treasure to bury it standing up."

The gods had no choice. But as they agreed, they noticed the otter skin mysteriously growing bigger and bigger. The cunning king of the dwarfs was using his magic to get as much gold as possible!

"Two of you must stay here," King Hreidmar demanded, rubbing his hands. "Now, who is going to go and find me some treasure?"

Loki smiled behind his beard. He knew exactly who had a treasure trove *and* where to find that person.

"I'll go," he said.

First, Loki visited the sea goddess Ran and borrowed her magic fishing net. Then he set off to a certain waterfall to go fishing for a very special catch.

It wasn't long before Loki spotted and caught a trout, one that was bigger and shinier than the other fish. He watched gleefully as it struggled in Ran's net. Finally, the trout changed into a dwarf. He was called Andvari.

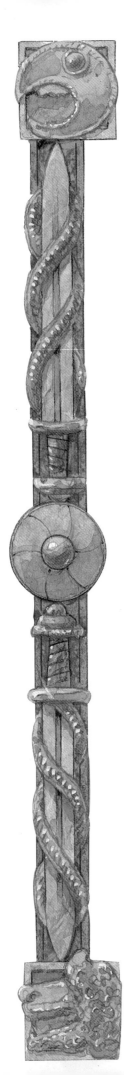

Now Loki knew that Andvari had a huge hoard of hidden gold. He forced the dwarf to give up his whole treasure trove in return for his freedom. Loki stuffed the riches into a huge sack and didn't let Andvari keep a single thing— not even the ring he wore around his arm.

"May trouble and sorrow come to all who keep it!" cursed the unhappy dwarf, as Loki stuffed the golden band into his pocket and hurried away.

Odin and Hoenir sighed with relief when they saw Loki returning, dragging the bulging sack. Bit by bit the gods filled the otter skin with treasure and covered it with gold. But King Hreidmar just chuckled wickedly.

"The otter is not yet covered up!" he sneered.

Loki gasped and peered at the shining pile. Sure enough, the tip of one whisker was poking out of the top.

In a panic, Loki turned his treasure sack inside out.

It was quite empty.

Then Loki remembered Andvari's arm-ring.

"I have just the thing," he said, carefully laying the band of bad luck into place. Then the gods hurried away, leaving the greedy king admiring his hoard....

It wasn't long before the curse of Andvari's ring began to work. The king's son Fafnir grew jealous as he watched his selfish father counting his coins and jewels.

Fafnir was so jealous that, one night, he killed his father. Then he stole the treasure and turned himself into a fearsome dragon so that he could guard it forever.

Regin, the king's last son, fled to Midgard when he saw what his evil brother had done. But Fafnir did not live happily ever after. The curse of the ring was not over. Years later, Regin's son tracked down his dragon uncle and killed him on the spot.

Regin himself lived the rest of his life with humans in the land of Midgard. He shared with them his dwarf secrets, which are still important to us today—how to build homes and make tools, and how to farm the land. The people of Midgard were truly grateful for this gift of wisdom—a treasure far more precious than gold.

TYR THE HERO

Long, long ago, women had beards. Mountains had roots.
Birds could spit, fish could speak, and cats' footsteps were
loud and clear. But not any more. All these things were
taken from the world of Midgard to make a very special
spell. A spell that the gods needed to keep them out of
great danger....

It all began when Odin, the chief of the gods, found
out that the trouble-making god Loki had fallen in love
with a giantess, and that they had three monstrous
children. There was Jormungand, a huge snake with a
forked tongue and poisonous fangs. There was Hel,
a woman who was only alive from the waist upward.
Her lower body and legs were cold and dead. And there
was Fenris, a massive wolf cub with bristling hair,
drooling jaws, and fierce yellow eyes.

Odin was worried. The giants hated the gods and
wanted the gods' kingdom, Asgard, for themselves.
If Loki's horrible children grew up to fight on the
giants' side, the gods would be in serious trouble....

Odin thought it would be wrong to kill the
monsters. After all, their father was one of the gods.

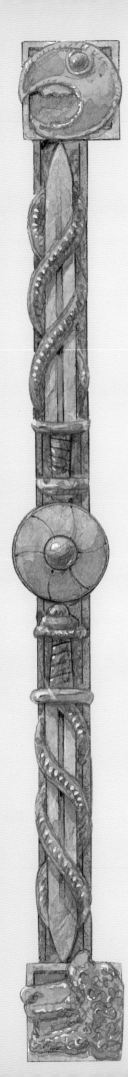

But he had to do something. So Odin swooped down from Asgard and grabbed the slithering serpent. With a great roar, he hurled him far, far away. Jormungand splashed into the sea, where he grew big enough to circle the universe and bite his tail.

Next, Odin found Hel and cast her deep into the earth. Down and down she sank until she reached the dark underworld of Niflheim. There she became the queen of the dead.

Finally, Odin caught Fenris the wolf cub and dragged the howling, struggling beast back home to Asgard.

The other gods and goddesses were horrified.

"Why have you brought this monster pup here?" one of them cried, backing away from the beast.

"It is said that a wolf will kill you," another god reminded the chief.

"We should put it to death!" someone yelled.

"Stop!" bellowed Tyr, the god of war. "Odin brought Fenris here, so we should treat him as our guest."

"But who will look after the brute?" argued a god.

Tyr looked at the snarling, snapping mass of hair, muscle, and teeth.

"I will," he said.

From that day forward, the fearless Tyr fed Fenris.

In his care, the giant cub grew to be a giant wolf.
A giant wolf on the loose in Asgard! The time came
when everyone felt they would sleep much better at
night if Fenris was tied up. So the gods and goddesses
took an especially strong chain and went to trick him.

"Fenris, let's play a game," the warriors suggested.
"We'll tie you up and you show us how powerful you
are by bursting free."

They never thought that Fenris would break the
mighty chain. But the wolf just gave a little shake, as
if he was drying himself, and a shower of metal pieces
flew from his coat.

The shocked citizens of Asgard pretended to
be delighted.

"Oh, well done!" they cried nervously. "Bravo!"

The gods and goddesses soon brought an even
stronger chain. Once again, Fenris burst out of its
thick links as if they were loops of thread.

Everyone was horrified—even Odin. He sent
Skirnir, a faithful servant of the god Frey, to the
land of the dwarfs to ask for their help.

When the king of the dwarfs heard what a danger
the wolf Fenris might be, he set his very best dwarf
craftsmen to work at once.

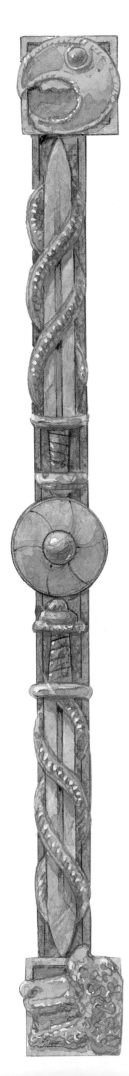

They brewed up a powerful spell using the beards of women, the roots of the mountains, the spit of birds, and the voice of every fish in the oceans. Then they added the sound of cats' footsteps, and their work was done.

Finally Skirnir showed Odin what the dwarfs had made. It was a rope as smooth and soft as a silk ribbon.

"The dwarfs say that no one can break this," Skirnir told Odin.

The chief of the gods went straight to Fenris and challenged him to play the game. The wolf was curious when he saw the rope and sniffed it nervously.

Hmmm, thought Fenris. *This might be a trick.*

He licked his lips.

"I shall only play if someone puts their hand in my mouth," Fenris said.

A shocked murmur ran around the waiting crowd.

"That way, we trust each other. I trust you to untie me if I can't break free. And you trust me not to bite."

Everyone gasped as Tyr stepped forward. He thrust his hand into the mouth of the animal he had looked after.

"Bind him!" he ordered.

Soon, the wolf's body and legs were tightly crisscrossed with the rope. Fenris looked deep into his friend's eyes. Then he began to struggle.

He heaved and strained. He thrashed his head and arched his back. But the knots grew tighter and tighter.

Finally, with a howl of rage, Fenris snapped his jaws—and his razor-sharp teeth sliced off Tyr's hand.

Perhaps it was an accident, because the wolf was straining so hard. Maybe Fenris bit down deliberately, because he was so upset at being betrayed by his friend. The brave Tyr never knew. But that is how the mighty god of war came to have only one hand.

As for Fenris, he is still tied up. Only at the end of time will he be set free to take his revenge....

GERDA THE BEAUTIFUL

When the night sky is starry and clear, the people of the icy northern lands look up and gasp in amazement, for they can see strange colored lights shimmering in the heavens. They know that the magical glow is the beauty of Gerda, the frost giantess. And they remind each other of her story, a tale of love at first sight....

Odin, the chief of the gods, has a great throne from which he sees everything that goes on in all nine worlds of the universe. Once Frey, the god of summer, dared to sit in it. Suddenly Frey found he could see far into the distance. His eyes fell upon the most beautiful woman he had ever seen—Gerda, the frost giantess.

From that moment on, Frey could think of nothing else but Gerda. He couldn't eat or drink or sleep. Finally he formed a desperate plan.

"Will you do something very difficult and dangerous for me?" Frey asked his most trusted servant, Skirnir. "Will you go to the land of the giants and bring back Gerda to be my bride?"

The faithful servant agreed at once.

"Take my magic sword to help you," Frey told Skirnir.

"It flies through the air and attacks by itself. And ride my horse. He is afraid of nothing."

Lastly, Frey laid two bundles in Skirnir's hands.

"These are very special presents," he said. "Surely they will win my lovely Gerda's heart."

Skirnir rode like the wind for a whole day and night, only stopping to pick up a magic wooden staff he saw lying on the road. Gerda's hall was circled by an enchanted fire and protected by two huge guard dogs. But Frey's brave horse leaped over the flames and tore past the snarling hounds. He carried Skirnir right into the palace, taking Gerda completely by surprise.

The beautiful frost giantess was shocked to hear that the god of summer wanted to marry her. Skirnir unwrapped the first of Frey's gifts.

"Frey has sent you eleven golden apples," he explained. "If you eat them, you will stay young forever."

"Why would I want to stay young, if everyone I love is going to grow old and die?" said Gerda sadly.

Skirnir didn't give up, but unwrapped the second gift.

"This is the arm-ring of Odin himself," he said proudly. "Frey wants you to have it."

"How lovely!" Gerda sighed, watching the gems sparkle. "But I'm a giant. It wouldn't even fit on my little finger!"

Skirnir began to feel a little annoyed, and his hand went to Frey's magic sword.

"If I draw this blade, it will fly to your neck and slice off your head!" the servant threatened.

"Then Frey will never have me!" Gerda laughed. "And my father will pull you to pieces, bit by bit."

All Skirnir had left was the wooden staff. It didn't look as splendid as the other things, but Skirnir knew its magic was very strong.

"Unless you marry Frey, I will put a terrible curse on you," Skirnir shouted, holding the staff up high. "I will turn you into an ugly hag! I will make you as hungry as a wolf, but all food will taste like salt. I will send you to the world of the dead, to watch the souls in torment...."

Gerda sighed a heavy sigh.

"Then I suppose I must agree," she said quietly. "But Frey must allow me nine days and nights to prepare myself."

When Skirnir told Frey the news, he was overjoyed. Each of the nine days of waiting seemed to him as long as a whole cold, dark month of winter.

But Gerda's arrival was worth waiting for. As soon as the frost giantess reached Asgard and looked into Frey's eyes, she fell just as much in love with him as he was with her. And they have lived together happily ever since.

THOR'S LOST HAMMER

The people of Midgard trembled inside their houses.
Huge, black storm clouds blotted out the heavens.
The rumbling of thunder crashed across the skies,
and bolts of lightning blazed down toward the earth.

"Thor is angry," the terrified people whispered to
each other.

The great thunder god was more furious than they
could imagine. Someone had stolen his magic hammer,
Mjollnir. Thor was sure that he had gone to sleep with
the precious weapon safely tucked inside his belt. But
when he woke up, it had gone.

"Loki!" Thor roared, calling for his friend the mischief-
maker. "Have you stolen my hammer?"

"I wouldn't dare!" Loki protested. "But I will help
you find it."

While Thor yelled and stamped, Loki hurried away to
find Freya, the goddess of beauty. She had a magic feather
cloak in which she could fly as a bird. And Loki wanted
to borrow it....

Soon the crafty god was soaring high above the earth
on eagle's wings. His sharp eyes scanned the ground.

There was no sign of Thor's hammer anywhere.

Then Loki's keen ears caught the sound of voices on the wind. Voices boasting of how the giant Thrym had spotted Mjollnir lying on the ground next to the sleeping Thor and couldn't resist taking it.

Loki hovered over the land of the giants until he spotted Thrym far below him.

"Hello there, Loki!" the smirking giant called out, as Loki came swooping down. "How are things in Asgard?"

"Things are very bad—and well you know it!" Loki said sternly. "Where have you hidden Thor's hammer?"

"Somewhere that noisy god will never find it!" Thrym chuckled. "And I will only give it back on one condition—that I marry the beautiful goddess Freya."

Loki flew back to Thor as fast as he could.

"I know who has your hammer, but I haven't been able to get hold of it," Loki told his sulking friend.

"Who's got it?" bellowed Thor. "Hammer or no hammer, I'll beat the thief to a pulp!"

"Calm down!" urged Loki. "The giant Thrym has Mjollnir, and he will give it back if Freya marries him. All we have to do is persuade her to agree...."

But Loki was speaking to thin air. Thor had already charged away to find the goddess.

"Get yourself ready, Freya!" he blurted out. "You're going to the land of the giants to be married, so I can have my hammer back."

"Oh, really!" Freya said. Her eyes flashed with anger. "Well, you can rage as much as you like, but you're not going to bully me into marrying some clumsy giant—and that's final!"

The furious Thor went back to Loki.

"Now I've lost Mjollnir *and* upset Freya," the thunder god shouted. "Have you got any more great ideas?"

For once, Loki was stuck. It was Heimdall, the guardian of the rainbow bridge between Asgard and Midgard, who came up with an idea. Thor and Loki didn't like the sound of it one little bit. But neither of them had a better plan.

That night, Thor's mighty war chariot rumbled out of Asgard with a bride and bridesmaid inside. But the blushing bride wasn't Freya. It was the highly embarrassed thunder god disguised in wedding clothes. And the bridesmaid was Loki, dressed in a gown and carrying a bunch of flowers.

The giant Thrym was delighted when he saw the chariot coming. He ran all over his house giving orders to his servants.

"Quick! Prepare a magnificent banquet and send out invitations!" he yelled. "Freya must have the best wedding feast ever."

By the time the two gods arrived, Thrym was so excited that he didn't notice how big and hairy they were. But later on at the feast, the size of his bride's appetite shocked him. Not only did Freya wolf down a whole ox and an entire tray of fish, she washed down her food with two barrels of beer.

"I've never seen a girl eat and drink like that!" the giant exclaimed.

Quick as a flash, Loki piped up, "Freya has been looking forward so much to meeting you that she hasn't been able to eat a thing for days."

Thrym looked lovingly at his bride and bent to kiss her.

But the instant the giant drew close to her, he jumped
back in horror.

"Her eyes! They're all red and angry!" he cried.

Once again, Loki saved the day.

"Freya's been longing to come here so badly that
she hasn't been able to sleep at night," he trilled.

Thrym sighed with happiness and got to his feet
to make a speech.

"Giants and giantesses," he began. "I am the luckiest
being in the universe. I never dared hope that Freya
would love me. I thought she would only marry me
so that Thor could have his hammer back. But it's clear
that her feelings are as strong for me as my feelings are
for her. And now it's time to keep my part of the bargain.
Bring in Mjollnir—a wedding present for my bride!"

As soon as Thor felt his hammer in his hands,
he ripped off his disguise and sprang to his feet with
a terrible roar.

Thrym just had time to gasp, "A trick!" before the
thunder god killed him with one blow. Seconds later,
every other giant at the wedding feast lay dead too.
And to this day, no one has ever been foolish enough to
take Thor's bone-crushing weapon away from him again.

A Deadly Trick

The ordinary people of Midgard tried to live brave and noble lives, just like the warrior gods and goddesses of Asgard. The humans knew that if they died bravely in battle, they would be taken up to Valhalla, the Hall of Dead Heroes. There, they would enjoy fighting each other all day long. Each night they would feast together, while poets told of their bold deeds.

But many humans died of old age, accident, or sickness, and not in the glory of battle. These people went down to the underworld of Niflheim with its terrible queen, Hel. And it wasn't just humans who lived in dread of the deep, silent kingdom of the dead. So did the gods and goddesses themselves....

Odin, the chief of the gods, and Frigga, his wife, had many children. Among them were twins called Hoder and Balder. They were both gentle, kind boys, although they looked the exact opposite of each other. Hoder had been blind from birth and wandered around Asgard in darkness. Balder was the god of light, with a shining face and glowing hair. Everyone loved Balder the best. They couldn't help it. He spread happiness wherever he went.

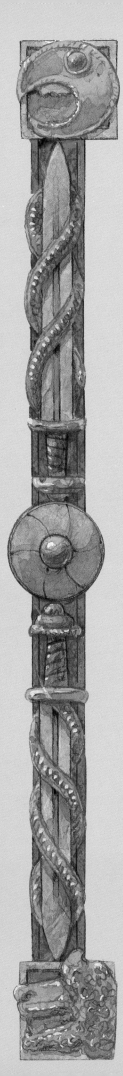

But then a change began to come upon Balder. His smile faded and his eyes lost their sparkle. His sweet wife, Nanna, often found him sitting on his own, lost in troubled thoughts. At night, Balder would shout out and toss and turn in nightmares.

Balder had become afraid of death.

When his mother, Frigga, found out what was wrong, she decided to use her great powers to help her favorite son. She traveled the universe and asked everything in it to swear a solemn oath not to cause Balder any harm. Frigga spoke to the earth, the rocks, and the sea. She called to each insect, fish, animal, and bird. She talked to the flowers, the plants, and the trees, and also to the dwarfs, the elves, and the giants, and even each illness and disease. Every single thing vowed never to hurt so much as a hair on Balder's head.

All, that is, except for one sprig of mistletoe. Frigga only realized that she had left out the tiny green shoot when she was on her way back to Asgard.

Surely that one little stem couldn't hurt Balder, the exhausted queen thought to herself. And without stopping to speak to the mistletoe, she hurried on....

When Frigga explained to Balder that he was now safe, he cheered up and became his old self again.

The delighted gods and goddesses breathed a huge sigh of relief and celebrated by making up a new game.

They took Balder to the great Hall of Peace, to show that they meant no harm. Then they threw rocks and fired arrows at Balder, and tried to slash him with swords. Everyone laughed with joy—Balder loudest of all. For the rocks just bounced off him. The arrows seemed to lose their aim in mid-air. And the sword blades simply bent and buckled. Even Thor's magic hammer spun through the air and returned to the thunder god's hand without going near Balder. The god of light was left without a single scratch.

"Hooray for Balder!" the joyful gods and goddesses cried. "What a hero!"

Everyone was having far too much fun to notice that Loki the mischief-maker wasn't smiling. The more the gods and goddesses cheered and slapped Balder on the back, the more Loki felt unloved and left out. And the god of light looked even more handsome and healthy now that he was no longer afraid of death. Filled with hatred and jealousy, Loki crept away to plot against Balder....

Satisfied that her work had been done well, Queen Frigga took a walk through Asgard, humming to herself.

Suddenly she noticed a strange old woman standing nearby. Frigga greeted her warmly, and the two began to chat.

"Is it really true that there's nothing at all that can harm Balder?" the crone croaked.

"Everything in the universe has sworn not to hurt my fair son," the queen smiled. "Except for a little mistletoe plant to the west of Valhalla. And how can that do any harm?"

The old woman's eyes twinkled.

"Yes, how indeed?" she agreed, curtseying low. And she watched, grinning her toothless grin, as the queen continued her walk.

As soon as Frigga was out of sight, the old woman cast off her ragged cloak and changed back into her true form—it was Loki!

Without wasting a moment, he dashed away to find the mistletoe. It had grown much bigger since the queen had passed by. Loki cut a long stem, stripped off the leaves and berries, and carefully sharpened the point into a dart.

The evil Loki knew exactly where to find Balder. The other gods and goddesses never tired of hurling rocks and weapons at the god they couldn't harm.

Laughter rang out from the Hall of Peace all day long. Only Balder's brother, the blind god Hoder, wasn't joining in the sport. He hung back sadly, listening to the fun going on without him.

"Why don't you take a shot like everyone else?" Loki whispered in Hoder's ear. "Take hold of this twig and I'll guide your hand."

Hoder's dark face brightened.

"Oh, I'd love to join in!" he said gratefully. "Thank you."

And Hoder let the cunning god help him throw the deadly dart at his beloved brother.

At once, Hoder realized that something had gone dreadfully wrong. There was a stunned silence as the dart entered Balder's chest, piercing him through the heart. Then a thud as the god hit the ground. Next came Nanna's screaming, and weeping and wailing from all the gods around. And finally came the noise of Loki's guilty footsteps running away, leaving Asgard forever.

Poor Hoder was beside himself with grief. He knew that he had somehow caused a terrible accident. His brother Balder had been killed.

And worst of all, because Balder hadn't died bravely in battle, his soul would soon be on its way to the darkness of Niflheim, the horrible kingdom of the dead....

LOKI'S PUNISHMENT

The day Balder died, a shadow was cast over the land of Asgard. The grim-faced gods and weeping goddesses carried his body down to the seashore, where Ringhorn, the greatest of all longboats, was waiting on the sand. Balder's friends loaded the splendid ship with everything the god of light would need in the underworld: fine robes, precious jewelry, powerful weapons, golden plates, and silver goblets.

Then Balder's sorrowing father, Odin, stepped forward. His two ravens, Hugin and Munin, clung to his slumped shoulders as his blue cloak billowed out around him in the breeze. Odin took off his magic arm-ring, Draupnir, and laid it next to his beloved son as a last gift.

Then it was time for Balder's wife, Nanna, to say goodbye. But as she bent over to give Balder one last kiss, her heart broke and she died. Filled with new grief, the gods and goddesses laid Nanna's body next to her husband's.

All that remained now was for the mighty longboat to be pushed into the water and set on fire.

The ship was so heavy that the gods could not move it alone. They called for the giantess Hyrrokkin, who came riding on a huge wolf, with snakes for reins. Using her great strength, she heaved the ship into the waves. The splash was so loud that it was heard in all nine worlds of the universe.

Queen Hel heard the sound in her dank kingdom. *Balder will soon be with me*, she thought triumphantly.

Thor stepped aboard the floating ship and raised his magic hammer high. He bellowed a charm so that the dead Balder would travel safely to the underworld. Then the thunder god smashed down his hammer and sparks flew all around. The longboat caught fire.

The burning ship began to drift away on the dark ocean. But it wasn't just the gods and goddesses of Asgard who watched it go. Giants were there too, as well as the Valkyries, the winged women who choose fallen warriors to live in glory in Valhalla. Even dwarfs and elves had come to mourn the god of light.

"Is there anyone who will try to save my beautiful son?" wept Queen Frigga, as the longboat disappeared over the horizon in a blaze of flames. "Will someone make the dreaded journey to Niflheim and plead with Hel to allow Balder to return to the land of the living?"

Hermod, the messenger of the gods, accepted the challenge. There wasn't a moment to lose. He put on his helmet, leapt upon Odin's eight-legged horse, and in a flash he was gone.

Hermod rode through days and nights without pausing for breath, and at last he reached the border of Hel's kingdom. A ghostly bridge lay before him in the mist, hanging over the River of the Dead. Hermod urged the horse forward, and the hammering of its many hoofs rang out in the silence.

Finally the horse leapt into the gloom of Hel's palace itself. On and on the fearless horse and rider raced through the dark chambers, until they reached the great hall.

The awful queen of the dead was seated at a huge dining table piled with foul and decaying food. Hermod climbed off his panting horse and knelt at Hel's rotting feet. He looked up into her ghastly eyes.

"Beings from all nine worlds are grieving for Balder," the brave messenger told Hel. "Please, allow him to ride back to Asgard with me."

"Hmmmmm," said Hel thoughtfully, drumming her bony fingers on the arm of her throne. "Very well. If all things everywhere—both living and dead—shed tears for the dead Balder, then he can return to the world of the light."

Hermod set out on his return journey with new hope in his heart. Balder had been so good-hearted and generous, surely all of creation would weep for him.

The desperate Queen Frigga sent out messages once again asking all things everywhere to obey her. And the whole universe began to cry. Water oozed out of soil and rock and metal. Tears ran from the eyes of insects, birds, and animals. Sap poured from trees and plants. The sound of wailing rose from the human world of Midgard, and Queen Hel's subjects howled in the kingdom of the dead. All the dwarfs and elves shed tears for Balder in their mysterious secret worlds.

Even the giants forgot their quarrels with the warriors of Asgard and wept great rivers of tears.

But Balder did not appear.

As the gods and goddesses stood in stunned silence, the sound of giant laughter came floating to them on the wind. Far away, in a distant corner of the giant kingdom of Jotunheim, a giantess called Thokk was enjoying their sorrow.

"I will not weep for Odin's favorite son!" she cackled. "Let the god of light stay forever in the darkness of the underworld!"

And so it was that Hel kept Balder in her kingdom.

But Odin suspected evil at work. Something about Thokk's voice had seemed familiar, and suddenly he realized why.

"That wasn't a giantess!" he gasped in horror. "It was Loki in disguise!"

The furious gods set out at once to find the wicked trickster.

But Loki was already on the run. He knew that the gods would never forgive him for what he had done, and that they would come looking for him. So he hid himself away at the top of a high mountain in the land of Midgard, in a house next to a waterfall.

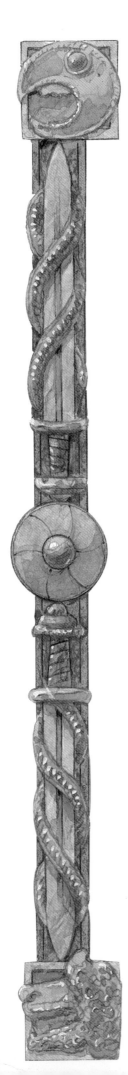

There, Loki thought he was safe. He could see for miles all around, and if he ever spied someone coming, he planned to turn himself into a salmon and hide under the silvery, tumbling waters.

But Loki's luck had finally run out.

One day Odin, Thor, and Kvasir found the cunning god's hideout. It was empty, but they soon figured out where Loki must be. The three gods remembered how Loki had once used a net to trap the disguised dwarf Andvari, and they quickly made a net of their own.

Now it was Loki's turn to be the catch of the day. Odin, Thor, and Kvasir went fishing, and before long, a slippery salmon was wriggling in Thor's hands, changing back into Loki before their very eyes.

Loki knew that he could expect no mercy. The gods dragged him away to a cave deep below a mountain. They tied him up with ropes made from the flesh of one of his own sons, then magically changed them into iron. An enormous snake was fixed above Loki's head. Drip . . . drip . . . drip . . . venom from the snake's fangs began to fall onto Loki's face. The drops burned into his skin and he howled in pain.

The gods closed their ears to his screams and left the cave forever. But Loki's wife, Sigyn, hurried to his side.

She is there in the cave to this day, holding a bowl above Loki's head to catch the snake's burning poison. When the bowl is full, Sigyn has to turn aside to empty it. In that split second, a drop of venom lands on Loki's skin and he moans in agony. The echoes of his pain go rippling underground, causing earthquakes in the world of Midgard.

Those who can see into the future say that Loki's punishment will not finish until the great battle at the end of time. Then at last he will be set free to fight with the giants against the mighty warrior gods and goddesses of Asgard....

INDEX

Alfheim, land of the light elves 5
Andvari, a dwarf 15, 16, 46
Asgard, land of the warrior gods 5, 7, 11, 13, 19-21, 32, 35, 41

Balder, god of light 35-39, 41-45

dwarfs 5, 13-17, 21-22, 36, 42, 44

Fafnir, a dwarf 14, 16, 17
Fenris, a wolf 19-23
Frey, god of summer 25-27
Freya, goddess of beauty 29-31
Frigga, wife of Odin 35-38, 42, 44

Gerda, frost giantess 25-27
giants 5, 7-11, 13, 19, 25-27, 30-33, 36, 42, 45, 47

Heimdall, a gatekeeper god 31
Hel, queen of the dead 19-20, 35, 39, 42-45
Hermod, messenger of the gods 43-44
Hoder, brother of Balder 35, 39
Hoenir, brother of Odin 13-16
Hreidmar, king of the dwarfs 14-17, 21
Hyrrokkin, a giantess 42

Jormungand, a sea-serpent 5, 19-20
Jotunheim, land of the giants 5, 7-11, 13, 30-33, 45

Loki, half-giant, half-god 7-11, 13-16, 19, 29-33, 37-39, 45-47

Midgard, land of humans 5, 7, 13, 17, 19, 29, 35, 44, 45, 47
Mjollnir, Thor's magic hammer 7, 29-31, 33, 37, 42
Muspell, land of fire 5

Nanna, wife of Balder 36, 39, 41
Nidavellir, land of the dwarfs 5
Nidhogg, a dragon 5
Niflheim, kingdom of the dead 5, 20, 35, 39, 42-45

Odin, chief of the gods 13-16, 19-22, 25-26, 35, 41, 43, 46

Ran, goddess of the sea 15
Ratatosk, a squirrel 5
Regin, a dwarf 14, 17
Ringhorn, a longboat 41-42

Sigyn, wife of Loki 46-47
Skirnir, a servant 21-22, 25-27
Svartalfheim, land of the dark elves 5

Thialfi, a servant 7, 9-10
Thor, god of thunder 7-11, 29-33, 37, 42, 46
Thrym, a giant 30, 32-33
Tree of Life 5
Tyr, god of war 20-23

Valhalla, Hall of Dead Heroes 35
Valkyries, winged women 42
Vanaheim, land of gods who make things grow 5

48